Bedtime Stories for Amazing Boys

An Uplifting Collection of Stories for Giving Young Boys
Ambition, Confidence, Courage, and Resilience

Hayden Fox

Table of Contents

A Note for Readers Young and Old

This is a book about dinosaurs, which is pretty awesome. Everything about dinosaurs is larger than life, including their names. If you see a name that's too long to pronounce, don't get discouraged. You will find all the characters in these stories on the cast list, and you'll also find that the list includes a handy pronunciation guide. If you're still struggling, slowly count the syllables or look for familiar vowel sounds and use that to guide you through saying their names the first few times. Whether this is your first time reading about dinosaurs or you are a lifelong fan, the pronunciation guide will help you talk about dinosaurs like a pro.

The only thing harder than pronouncing dinosaur names is growing up, and these stories will help there too. You'll read stories about honesty, compassion, bravery, and resilience as dinosaurs try to be the best dinosaurs they can be: good to their friends, and good to themselves too.

Growing up (and being a grown-up!) is about trying new things, succeeding, failing, learning, and growing from all of those experiences. These stories are designed to help readers find encouragement, learn some life lessons, and have a dinosaur-sized ton of fun along the way.

Enjoy!

The Dinosaurs of the Tooth and Nail Tar Pit

Tracer Triceratops *(Try-Sare-A-Tops):* A young, three-horned dinosaur who loves playing with his friends, meeting new people, and talking as much as he can.

Stinger Styracosaurus *(Sty-Rack-A-Sore-Us):* Tracer's friend, a slightly bigger dinosaur with many horns who just wants to stay out of trouble.

Toodles the Pterodactyl *(Tear-Oh-Dak-Tuhl):* Just hatched. Can't talk yet. Loves flying and is very good at playing tag.

Stanley Stegosaurus *(Steh-Guh-Saw-Rhus):* Just started Stegosaurus school. He's excited about it, but he has a rather strange pink plate instead of an all-red one like everyone else, and he's worried someone might notice.

Star Stegosaurus: A small and cheerful dinosaur who is happy to be in school and looking to make new friends. Also a good painter.

Mr. Thag: A very, very old Stegosaurus. He's been a teacher for a long time, but he still loves every student.

Parsnip the Pachycephalosaurus *(Pack-E-Sef-A-Lo-Sore-Us):* Always wanted to be an inventor, so that's what he did. Like most inventors, some of his inventions work out great, but most of them are just really good tries.

Bertie Brontosaurus *(Brr-On-Toe-Sore-Us):* A friendly botanist who never tires of tasty vegetables.

Tank the Tyrannosaurus Rex *(Tie-Ran-Oh-Sore-Us Rex):* His first love is protecting the outdoors and making sure everyone who lives near him is safe and happy. His second love is donuts.

Zandelmandechar the Sea Turtle: Had to tell everyone how to pronounce his name (*Zan-Del-Man-Deh-Char*) until he got exasperated and started going by Zan. Really, really, really loves naps.

Grandpa Bachaelandafangoriouslinealmarkasius: Zan's Grandpa, a giant sea turtle. Not even trying to pronounce this one. Call him Grandpa B.

Aerothea the Great, a Quetzalcoatlus *(Ket-Suhl-Co-At-Luhs):* The greatest, biggest, and mightiest of all flying prehistoric animals. Knows she is the biggest and mightiest, too. Prefers to be alone.

The Terrible Tar Monster of Doom

The Tooth and Nail Tar Pit was an excellent place to explore. Tracer Triceratops and his friend Stinger Styracosaurus went there as often as their parents would let them. They found all manner of cool things there: shiny rocks, slimy moss, old bones, strange flowers, and more. You had to be careful around the tar and avoid the muck as much as you could, but otherwise it was great fun. Plus, the tar pit was delightfully stinky, which meant not too many other dinosaurs were around. Most days, Tracer and Stinger had the tar pit to themselves.

Or so they thought.

Tracer walked along the edge of the tar pit, carefully digging in the dirt with one of his horns to search for lost treasure. Stinger did the same, although he was louder and less careful with his digging. The popping bubbles from the pit offered their own sort of background noise, but today, Tracer thought he heard something different.

"Shhh," Tracer said to Stinger.

"I'm not being that loud!" Stinger said. "Anyway, being loud is why we're out here. We play at home until my mom tells me that I have to play outside if I'm going to be so noisy and bang around so much. Then we come here. This place is made for being noisy." He illustrated his point with a loud bellow that echoed around the tar pits.

Tracer gave him a look, and Stinger stopped to listen. Was that a tiny... squawk? The noise was so quiet that they almost wondered if they were imagining it, until suddenly they heard it again. They crept toward the sound, taking care to be much quieter than usual.

They pushed through some tall grass and saw it: a nest with a tiny bald hatchling, all alone among some still-unhatched eggs. But that wasn't all—it was right on the edge of the tar pit. One little move and that little guy was going to be in big trouble.

"What do we do?" Tracer asked.

"I think we go down there and get him," Stinger said.

Tracer looked at the ground between them and the hatchling. It was stable in the tall grass where they were, but then quickly turned into a sandy, muddy mess closer to the edge of the tar. There were splatters of tar on the sand as well—some patches were even still steaming. It looked incredibly unstable.

"I'll go," Tracer said. "I'm smaller, so maybe I won't get stuck."

"I can come with...," Stinger said absentmindedly, but Tracer noticed that Stinger was looking past him out into the tar. "Do you know what that is?" Stinger asked.

Tracer turned and looked out into the lake of tar. At first, he didn't see anything. It was bubbling and splattering like it always did. Maybe there were a few more bubbles than usual? But then he saw it, way out near the center—a bubble of tar rising out of the lake, bigger than he had ever seen. And it was still growing.

Tracer jumped through the weeds onto the barren area next to the pit and ran toward the hatchling. They needed to get out of there, and fast. However, he wasn't going to leave the hatchling behind.

He made it almost all the way to the nest, but then one of his feet sank into the muddy ground and stuck fast. He looked over to the tar pit again and saw that the giant bubble wasn't a bubble at all. It was the giant, spiny shell of some sort of... tar pit monster? Tracer couldn't tell exactly, but he sensed

that whatever was rising from the tar pit was big trouble.

Stinger, though, wasn't about to leave his friend behind, and he was there in a flash. He yanked Tracer out of the muck, and they dashed over to the nest. The hatchling inside seemed like a Pterodactyl, but it was hard to tell when they were this young. Right now, it just looked like a pink-gray lump with a long beak.

The boys scooped up the Pterodactyl, nest and all. One of the eggs started to roll out, but Tracer saved it just in time. They scrambled away from the tar pit onto more solid ground. The baby Pterodactyl didn't seem so quiet anymore. In fact, it was screeching in protest, but Tracer and Stinger barely noticed as they looked out at the lake. They could see a head and a long neck rising out of the tar, with the massive shell behind it. It was shining black and covered in the sticky tar. The boys knew that the tar was very hot and very dangerous, and they didn't know any dinosaur that would be safe touching it—let alone living in it.

They sprinted away as fast as they could. The eggs jostled and the baby cried out, but Tracer and Stinger kept everyone safe as they ran and ran, not stopping or looking back until the tar pit was well out of sight.

"I can't believe we made it, " Stinger gasped.

"We all did," Tracer said, panting. He looked down at the Pterodactyl and the yellow spotted eggs nestled beside it. "But I have the feeling whoever these eggs belong to isn't going to be too happy that they've gone missing."

"You're worried about some eggs right now?" Stinger asked. "Really? What about the terrible towering tar monster of doom we just saw? It's probably on its way here to eat everything in its path and cover everything with tar. I bet it breathes fire and has a roar that can knock down a forest and can fly and..."

Now, at the very least, Tracer was pretty confident the tar monster couldn't fly, because they didn't see any wings and flying would be awfully difficult when you were covered in tar. Still, the monster was bigger than anything Tracer had ever seen. He was no stranger to big creatures; after all, he was a dinosaur. But the tar monster was bigger than any dinosaur he'd ever seen. It was, well, monstrous.

"We're going to need some help," Tracer said.

The Pterodactyl chirped in agreement. With great effort, he flapped his wings until he lifted off, then flew around Tracer and Stinger playfully. He settled on Tracer's back, right behind his bony frill, and rode there as they walked home through the forest.

"Do you have a name?" Tracer asked.

The Pterodactyl let out a little squawk.

"I guess we'll have to give you one," Tracer said.

Stinger was still worried about the monster, although there was no sign they were being chased. The temptation to name their new friend was strong, though, so he joined in.

"I've never given someone a name before," Stinger said. "We should pick something scary and intimidating. Titan. Terror. Tarantula. Tar Face?"

The Pterodactyl growled in protest.

"Maybe something a little less intimidating," Tracer suggested. "What about Toodles?"

The Pterodactyl chirped happily and hopped up, flying in a circle and then settling down again.

"I think that settles it," Tracer said. "He'll be Toodles the Pterodactyl."

"I guess," Stinger said. He had really had his heart set on Tar Face. "Your mom is not going to be happy about us bringing home stray dinosaurs, no matter how cute his name is."

Tracer understood where his friend was coming from, but he thought otherwise. It was an emergency, and that would make his parents see things differently. They couldn't leave Toodles alone with the monster, and it was important to do what was right and protect others... even if his mom might be annoyed at having to set an extra spot at the dinner table. His mom had always told him that if something was important and he was honest about it, he wouldn't get in trouble for trying his best. He was proud of himself for rescuing Toodles. Now they needed to get back to his house, stop a rampaging tar pit monster, find Toodles' mom, and keep the eggs safe until they hatched. He was confident he'd done the right thing, but it was shaping up to be a very long day.

The Pink Plate Problem

It was Stanley Stegosaurus's first day of school. (Of course dinosaurs go to school—school is very important!) His mother had told him, many times, that it would be a fun, interesting, and safe day where he would meet a lot of new friends. The problem was, she had told him this so many times that he had started to wonder why she was trying so hard to convince him. As a result, he was nervous.

He was like other Stegosauruses in most ways. He liked eating grass and leaves, playing tag, reading books, and smashing things with his pointy tail. There was one way that he wasn't exactly like other Stegosauruses, though. He'd always noticed that the rest of his family had red plates on their backs, and he did too... except for one. The biggest, tallest plate—the one right in the middle of his back—was shockingly pink.

Stanley's mother had no idea why his plate was pink like that. She assured him that everyone was different, and people would barely notice. But, just like she'd done with the first day of school, she had reassured him so many times about it that he suspected the other dinosaurs would indeed notice.

His attempts to avoid school were fruitless, though. First, he pretended to lose his shoes, then he pretended to lose his backpack, and finally he pretended that he had an upset stomach. But his mother was as smart as she was kind, and she saw through his excuses easily. Like it or not—and he did *not*—the first day of school was going to happen.

His teacher was an ancient and wrinkly Stegosaurus named Mr. Thag. He was so old that when one of the other Stegosaurus kids asked how old he was, he answered fifty-one! Stanley didn't know anyone that old, except his Great-Grandmother Masie. Stanley was sure she was the oldest dinosaur in the world. Secretly, he thought Grandma Masie might be the oldest anything in the world, but his mother gave him a very pointed look if he ever brought it up.

Mr. Thag had one rule for his classroom: no nonsense. That disappointed Stanley and his classmates very much, because if there's one thing every young dinosaur loves, it's getting up to some nonsense. However, Mr. Thag was quite serious about it, so they all tried their best.

By the time it was recess, everyone except for Mr. Thag was ready to run around and play and make absolutely as much noise as possible. Stanley tried to join the dinosaurs playing tag, since it was his favorite game, but no one would chase him. Then he tried to join some dinosaurs playing football, but no one would pass him the ball. Finally, he tried swinging on the swings, but no one would give him a turn.

"I want a turn on the swings, please," Stanley asked one of the other boys in his class, who was using one of the swings. Stanley's voice was very small and quiet because he was very nervous.

The other Stegosaurus did not stop swinging. "Go away, weirdo! Weirdos don't get a turn on the swings. Weirdy weirdy weirdo," he yelled.

Stanley had never been called weird before, and he did not like the way it felt at all. He didn't think he was weird. He liked toys and playing and candy and video games, just like any other Stegosaurus boy. But he also didn't want to fight, so he went and sat by himself.

He watched the other Stegosauruses play. The ground shook thunderously as all the dinosaurs ran and jumped and climbed. Stanley wanted to join in, but he didn't know anyone and he didn't want to be called names again.

After a few minutes, another Stegosaurus walked up to him. He was small and thin for a Stegosaurus, with bright red plates and long, thin spikes on his tail. His tail swished around excitedly, even though he was standing still. He had a curious look in his eyes.

"Hi!" he said to Stanley.

"Hello," Stanley said. After being called weird, Stanley was cautious and feeling rather anxious about meeting someone new, but he wanted to be polite.

"I like your plates," the little Stegosaurus said. "My name is Star."

"That's a strange name for a Stegosaurus," Stanley said.

"Everybody has to be named something," Star said. "I like it."

Stanley suddenly realized that telling Star he had a strange name might make him feel bad, like Stanley had felt when the boy on the swings called him weird. He definitely did not want other dinosaurs to feel that way.

"I'm sorry," Stanley said. "I'm Stanley. I didn't mean to say your name was strange. I mean, it is a little strange, but I like it too. I don't think it's bad or anything, just different."

Stanley thought maybe it wasn't the best apology, since he had called Star strange again without meaning to. He knew it was important to apologize after making a mistake, though—even if he wasn't sure what to say and it made him feel embarrassed.

"That's okay!" Star said cheerfully. "My mom says my name is unique, not strange. She says sometimes how you say something is just as important as what you say. But she also makes me go to bed on time every night no matter how many different ways I ask to stay up, so it doesn't always work that way."

Stanley would have to ask his mother, but he suspected she, too, would insist that bedtime was non-negotiable.

"I don't like how you made fun of my plates," Stanley told Star, trying to explain his earlier rudeness.

"I didn't!" Star responded. "I like them. I think they're neat."

Stanley realized he had wrongly assumed he was being made fun of because he was so worried about being different and because another Stegosaurus had already been mean to him. Star probably realized the same thing and decided to be extra nice and careful with his new friend Stanley.

"I really do like your plates," Star assured him warmly. "I especially like your pink plate. I've never seen anything like it."

"I don't like it," Stanley replied. "I mean, I *did* like it, but now that I know people think it's weird, it makes me embarrassed."

Star kicked at the dirt. "I wish I had a plate like yours that was unique." His eyes brightened. "I have an idea! Will you help me decorate one of my plates so I can have a unique one, too?"

Coloring on yourself seemed like the sort of "nonsense" Mr. Thag would be very upset about, but Stanley was happy to make a friend. He hopped down from the bench and followed Star. Technically the dinosaurs were supposed to stay outside for recess, but they were allowed to come inside for emergencies. While this wasn't exactly an emergency, Star assured Stanley that as long as they mostly behaved, the adults wouldn't mind.

Star led the way to the art room, where a young teacher gave them a look but didn't indicate they should go back outside. Although she seemed curious, glancing over at them occasionally, she didn't say anything. Star banged around the room looking for supplies until finally the teacher decided she should intervene.

"Can I help you boys?" she asked.

"We need paint!" Star said. "And glitter! And glue and tape and crayons and colored paper and markers and glitter and scissors and fabric and..."

The teacher cut him off, looking worried that Star would list every art supply he had ever seen and maybe even some he hadn't. "That sounds like a lot of stuff," she said cheerfully. "And you said glitter twice."

"My mom says you should never miss a chance to use glitter," Star said.

The art teacher laughed. "Okay then. I'll get right on it."

She gathered everything up for them and set it up at a large table.

"What should we do first?" Stanley asked. New art supplies were always exciting, but he still wasn't sure what Star had in mind.

"Well, see that big plate, the one right in the middle of my back? We should paint that one blue," Star directed.

Stanley looked at the teacher, who gave them a shrug. If she was okay with it, he was okay with it. They mixed up some blue and purple and black paint until they had a deep, dark blue, just like the night sky.

"That's perfect," Star said.

They covered the plate on both sides with the blue paint, and it stood out spectacularly. And on top of that, they barely got any on Star's scales. It didn't look the same as Stanley's pink plate, but it was its own thing and Star was very happy with it.

"And now, the glitter!" he exclaimed.

Stanley quickly added the glitter while the paint was still wet, tossing it on and trying not to get too much everywhere else. He wasn't very good at keeping the glitter neat because he was so excited—but from the sparkles on the art room floor, Stanley guessed they weren't the first dinosaurs to get excited about glitter.

"It looks like stars," Stanley said cautiously. "Did I do it right?"

"Of course you did," Star cried. "It looks amazing! Stars for Star. I love it." He did an excited little spin and dance.

"Can we do one of my plates, too?" Stanley asked.

Star seemed even more excited to help his friend than he was about his own new plate. "Yeah, let's do it! What do you want me to put on there?"

"I don't really know," Stanley said. "I never thought about painting my plates before. I don't think my mom is as enthusiastic about glitter as yours is."

"Okay, it'll be a surprise then," Star told him excitedly.

Star got to work with all of his considerable energy. He left Stanley's special plate pink but painted on green lines and yellow swirls and purple dots, adding as many shapes and colors to the plate as he could. And of course, he added lots and lots of glitter. When he was done, it looked like someone had caught a rainbow in a jar, shaken it all up, and then dumped it out again. But Star had made sure the original pink was visible, too.

Stanley loved it. He still felt a little self-conscious, but it was the first time he had ever wanted to show off his special plate. The boys thanked the art teacher and got ready to leave. The teacher gave them a smile and looked at them patiently until they realized they should clean up the supplies before they left. Star and Stanley did the best job they could to pick everything up and put it away. The teacher thanked them and complimented them on their artwork, and they went back outside.

Recess ended a few minutes later, and when everyone came inside, other Stegosauruses started to whisper. Some dinosaurs thought their decorated plates were really cool, some thought they were strange, and some thought Stanley and Star would get in trouble.

When the boys got back to the classroom, Mr. Thag noticed immediately. But even though he was old and stern, he was very wise and had been teaching young dinosaurs for a long time. He could see that the paint was on Stanley's unique pink plate and correctly suspected that Stanley might be sensitive about it, so he didn't say anything.

Stanley's classmates were not as careful. One Stegosaurus raised his hand and said, "Mr. Thag, Stanley and Star got paint on themselves!"

Another Stegosaurus, the one who had called Stanley "weird" on the playground, raised his hand, too. "That's against the rules," he said. "They should get in trouble."

"I want one!" one of the other classmates said.

"Me too!" said another. Neither of them remembered to raise their hand.

Mr. Thag was quiet for a moment, and everyone waited to see if Stanley and Star would get punished. Would it be detention? Sent to the principal's office? Extra homework?

"Well, it appears we have some artists in the room," he said. "And plenty of others who would like to try their hand at being one. Art class was supposed to be tomorrow, but let me see if we can make a little schedule adjustment."

Mr. Thag left the room and the students buzzed with excitement. They all talked at once about what they'd paint on their own plates, or how they could decorate their horns or spikes or tails. Suddenly, the other Stegosauruses gathered around Stanley and Star—only this time it wasn't to be mean or call names, but to look at their designs and exclaim over the artwork.

Mr. Thag returned to the room, opened the door, and said gruffly, "Well, come on then. And be quiet in the hall."

The Stegosauruses followed Mr. Thag to the art room. It was very difficult to be quiet because they were so excited, but they tried their best. When they arrived, the art teacher had already set out the paint and other supplies at the tables so that everyone could gather around and work.

A Stegosaurus—even one who tries really hard—can't reach their own plates, so everyone had to take turns painting each other. Even Mr. Thag got in on the fun and had the art teacher paint several of his plates with pictures of rainbows, deserts, planets, and even a tiny Mr. Thag with a funny hat and a bow tie.

Painting their plates helped everyone listen to each other and bring out the things that made each Stegosaurus unique. Not only was painting really fun, but everyone also felt better about themselves and closer to their friends, too!

The Distraction Disaster

"Eggs get served for dinner; they don't get served dinner!"

That was Tracer's dad, bellowing loudly from the dining table. Tracer, his mom, his dad, Stinger, and Toodles the Pterodactyl had just settled down for dinner. Tracer knew his dad was just being gruff; after all, it wasn't too long ago that Tracer had come from an egg himself, so he figured his dad knew how to take care of eggs. He was pretty sure his dad would come around, once he'd had some time to think about it.

Toodles, who had already hatched out of his egg, did not know Tracer's dad. He squawked and chirped and hissed at the suggestion that his siblings should be turned into snacks.

"See?" Tracer's dad said. "Once they hatch, it's nothing but noise and extra mouths to feed."

Tracer's mom came over and set a bowl of berries on the table for Toodles, who started eating ravenously. It looked like Tracer's dad was going to speak up again, but Mrs. Triceratops gave him a friendly yet firm look, so he stayed quiet.

Mrs. Triceratops set two more bowls filled with large, rough leaves and some berries on the table. Tracer and Stinger started eating almost as fast as Toodles. It had been a very exciting day, and they were famished.

"Your friend can stay with us for a bit," Mrs. Triceratops said gently. "At least until we figure out where he belongs. I'm sure his parents are worried sick."

"I'm not sure he even knows his parents," Stinger said around a mouth full of leaves. "I think he just hatched."

"Well, moms and dads worry about their kids, even if the kids don't think about it much," Mrs. Triceratops said.

"That's a good point," Mr. Triceratops said. "Stinger, does your mother know where you are?"

"She knows I'm with Tracer, and she knows Tracer is very responsible." Stinger was good at saying nice things about Tracer, especially when they were barging in with eggs to take care of and wild stories of giant swamp monsters.

The swamp monster! Tracer was so tired and so hungry when they got home, he'd almost forgotten.

"Stinger, we have to tell them about the monster!" he blurted out.

The adults raised their eyebrows. In a world where giant dinosaurs with long fangs and sharp teeth were normal, it took a lot for something to be called a monster. Both Mr. and Mrs. Triceratops quietly thought the boys' imaginations were probably running a bit wild.

"There aren't any monsters in my kitchen," Mr. Triceratops pointed out. "But there is a baby Pterodactyl and a nest of eggs. I think we should talk about that, don't you?"

Tracer, who had slightly better manners than his friend, swallowed his food before he answered. "But we have to talk about the monster, 'cause that's why Toodles is here!"

"That Pterodactyl's mother is going to have a fit when she finds out we named her hatchling Toodles," Mrs. Triceratops said dryly.

But Mr. and Mrs. Triceratops were patient, and they listened while the boys told their story. Occasionally they would glance at each other or raise their eyebrows in surprise, but for the most part, they didn't try to interrupt.

When the boys finished, they looked at Tracer's parents with hesitation. They weren't sure just how the adults would respond.

"Well, that was quite the story," Mrs. Triceratops said. "I believe you think you saw a monster, and a monster mystery is not a job for children."

"Aw, mom!" Tracer whined. He was still scared of the swamp monster, but now that he had told his parents about it, he was curious, too. He wanted to go back and see it.

She held up a hand to silence his objections. "Maybe the thing you saw is dangerous, or maybe it's not. But it's my job to make sure that whatever you get up to, you're safe. Plus, there's a lot going on here, so I think we're going to split up to get it taken care of. I know you want to see a monster, but I'm going to give you another important job."

The boys pouted, but they listened.

"Your dad is going to get the park ranger so they can go and investigate the tar pit," Mrs. Triceratops instructed. "I'm going to go out and see if I can find Toodles' mother. I know I would be very upset if you boys went missing, so I'm sure she's pretty upset too. We can set up time to play with Toodles later, but first we should get him home where he belongs. So, I need you two here to look after Toodles and the eggs while we're gone. Can you do that?"

Of the three tasks, looking after some eggs seemed like the least interesting thing to do. On the other hand, at least Tracer and Stinger would get a chance to stay home by themselves, which felt like a lot of responsibility and wasn't something Tracer's mother had allowed before. So they agreed to watch Toodles and the eggs.

Tracer's parents left to attend to their tasks, and Tracer and Stinger set to work. They built an extra warm, cozy nest from some towels and even made sure to use the oldest towels so Tracer's parents wouldn't be upset. They put the original nest inside the new one and put it all on the table.

And then, they waited. Life is like that sometimes—the important thing to do isn't always the most exciting. They had thought they would spend the afternoon building things for the eggs, but they finished making the nest quickly. The house seemed very quiet and empty without Tracer's parents in it.

"What do we do now?" Stinger asked, watching the eggs intently. Toodles had covered himself up in the nest and was happily resting and enjoying the warmth, his eyes barely slitted open.

"Stare at them until they hatch, I guess?" Tracer said.

Both boys stared hard at the eggs. If any of them was going to hatch soon, they didn't show it. They stared and stared. It felt like a million years had passed, yet the eggs still hadn't hatched. Tracer looked at the clock. It had only been six minutes! Tracer's parents asked him to do a lot of things, and he was good at a lot of them. He was kind, he was thoughtful, and he was careful, at least as much as he was able to be. But the one thing it was incredibly difficult for Tracer to be was *patient.*

"Maybe it would be okay if we showed Toodles some of your toys," Stinger said. It seemed like he also felt that the last six minutes had lasted a million years.

Toodles hopped up and flew around a bit. He looked very excited to play with his new friends. Tracer figured that when you were only a day old, everything was new and exciting.

First, they tried to play catch, but it was hard because Toodles was too small to hold the ball. Then they tried to play with dolls and action figures, but those were too big for Toodles to hold, too. They played video games for a little while—those were Tracer and Stinger's favorite—but Toodles wasn't very good with the controller and had to watch instead of play. When Tracer and Stinger noticed Toodles wasn't having as much fun as they were, they decided to find something they could all do.

"Tag, you're it!" Stinger yelled, nudging Tracer and racing through the house.

Tracer chased after Stinger, and Toodles chased them both. The floor creaked and the furniture rattled as they ran through the house, and Toodles narrowly missed knocking over one of Mrs. Triceratops' prized glass figurines.

Tracer skidded to a stop and looked around at the books and dishes and knicknacks of all sorts that filled the house. "Um... maybe we should play outside if we're going to play tag," he said.

"You're still it!" Stinger said, dashing out the door and leaving it swinging wildly as he charged through. Toodles flew after him.

"We're supposed to be watching the eggs, though," Tracer said worriedly.

He was hoping his friends would have a good idea for how to do both, but they had already disappeared outside and were waiting to be tagged. Tracer looked at the eggs. Nothing about them had changed. They weren't going anywhere, right? He decided to follow Stinger and Toodles.

Tag was a lot of fun, especially with a flying dinosaur. Toodles swooped downward and then back up again. Tracer and Stinger jumped up after Toodles when they were trying to tag him, or looked for low places to hide when Toodles was chasing them. Originally, they played in the yard, but the more fun they had, the more they ran (or flew) and the farther they got from the house. They played all afternoon and had so much fun they lost track of time entirely, only noticing when it started to get dark.

"Maybe it's time to check the eggs again," Stinger said, huffing and puffing. He and Tracer were both out of breath from all the playing.

The three of them returned home, tired and ready to relax. But as soon as they opened the door, they knew they had made a gigantic mistake.

The house was in shambles. Chairs were knocked over. Pictures had fallen off the wall. An entire row of books was on the floor instead of in the bookshelf, and there were more than a few broken plates. Tracer looked at the table and saw that every single one of the eggs had hatched while they were away. A Pterodactyl who was definitely not Toodles zipped by overhead with one of Mrs. Triceratops' best hand towels in his beak.

Tracer and Stinger looked at each other. "Looks like we're playing some more tag," Tracer said.

They ran through the house chasing after the newly hatched baby Pterodactyls. Toodles chittered and chirped at his siblings to try and get them to calm down, but they were scared by the comparatively huge dinosaurs now thundering through the house around them. The boys had to jump over chairs and race up and down stairs. At one point Stinger tripped and fell through an end table, turning it into a ruined, splintery mess. But one by one, they caught the new babies and returned them to the nest, putting a giant colander over the top so they couldn't escape again. The Pterodactyls must have been flying around for a long time, because once they were back in the nest, they fell asleep almost immediately.

All of them were so tired! Toodles gave up immediately. He chirped apologetically at Tracer, lifted the colander enough to sneak under it, and curled up with his siblings, falling asleep as quickly as the others.

The boys knew they had made a grave mistake by abandoning their job, so they did their best to fix it.

Tracer's mother was fond of reminding him that it was okay to make messes, as long as you cleaned them up afterwards—and boy was this a big one. Although he and Stinger had been irresponsible by leaving the eggs unattended, they could be responsible now by cleaning up.

They worked hard despite how tired they were, and soon the house looked, well, better. Tracer wished he could call it "as good as new," but some of the broken things would need replacing. Some of them could be fixed, but that would be a job for Mr. Triceratops to help with since Tracer knew not to use tools without his parents.

He thought his mom and dad would see that he had tried his best, and they would be understanding about the mess. They might not be happy, but Tracer knew if he was honest and did everything he could to clean things up, his parents would help with the rest. He would do a better job to be more patient and perceptive in the future, but for now, everything was calm. Tracer and Stinger curled up next to the nest to make sure their new friends wouldn't cause any more trouble, and fell just as soundly asleep as the Pterodactyls.

The Super Sprayer: Prototype 9000

Parsnip the Pachycephalosaurus lived in a hole. He thought of it as a cave, but really, it was more like a stone basement without a house on top. Well, there used to be a house on top, but after it accidentally exploded for the fourth time, Parsnip decided he wasn't going to bother with rebuilding. So now he lived in a hole.

When he was young, Parsnip's mother told him he could be whatever he wanted to be. His mother probably thought he would be like the other boys and want to be something like a firefighter, a chef, a teacher, or a baseball player... maybe even something like a poet or a rock star, if he was feeling particularly fanciful. But Parsnip had a better idea: He wanted to be a scientist. Specifically, he wanted to be an inventor.

Inventors were not common among dinosaurs. To become an inventor, Parsnip needed to learn a lot of science and be very creative at the same time, and most dinosaurs simply had other things they would rather be doing. Not Parsnip, though—he was set on being the best inventor the world had ever seen!

His mother and his teachers thought it was adorable at first—something they could encourage for now and that he would grow out of when he was older. But instead of growing out of it, he grew into it! He tried his very best at science and never gave up, even though he wasn't always very good at it. In fact, he was so good at being resilient that many times throughout the years he would be called stubborn and hardheaded. "That boy," they would say, "has the hardest head out of anyone we've ever seen."

And he did. Pachycephalosaurus literally had the hardest head of any dinosaur, but later Parsnip learned that "hardheaded" also meant that he was stubborn. In spite of that, he didn't see himself that way—he saw himself as persistent. That meant sort of the same thing, but people used "persistent" when they wanted to be nice, and "stubborn" when they were frustrated. Parsnip decided that whenever someone called him stubborn, he would call himself persistent. He wanted to be nice to other people and he always tried his best, but he also decided he should treat himself just as nicely too. And so he did, and his life felt a lot better because of it. No matter how many times he made mistakes or blew up the house, he would encourage himself to keep trying, so long as he learned from his mistakes and avoided them in the future.

Today, he was putting the finishing touches on his latest invention, the Super Sprayer 9000. His previous invention, the Super Sprayer 8000, had sprung a leak, flooded the lab, and sent a huge geyser of water from the entrance of his hole high into the sky. Therefore, he determined either the pressure needed to be turned down or the hoses had to be reinforced. Hoses that were too firm and didn't have enough water pressure were the reason the Super Sprayer 7000 didn't work, so he'd tried soft hoses and a lot of water pressure for the Super Sprayer 8000; unfortunately, those didn't work either. Nevertheless, he was going to find a way to make his super sprayer work, even if the final version was the Super Sprayer 1,000,000.

That's why they called Parsnip a mad scientist: He never gave up, no matter how many times things went awry. He thought that being called a "mad scientist" was pretty unfair, just like when he'd been called "stubborn." He was rarely mad at all. In fact, he was often cheerful and always curious. So, whenever his science didn't quite go the way he wanted or even when it made all manner of chaos, he would laugh and say, "I'm a happy scientist!" as he watched everything fall apart in new and delightful ways.

He connected the main hose on the Super Sprayer 9000 to the rest of the machine so that water could be pumped into it from a large water tank—at least in theory. This time, though, the machine gave a halfhearted sputter and produced no water whatsoever.

"I'm going to need some help," Parsnip said to himself. He was a very intelligent dinosaur, and he knew that as long as he paid attention, he could learn something from everyone around him.

He climbed up the ladder and out of his hole into the morning sunshine. He often got so busy working that he forgot to check whether it was day or night—but if he had to choose, Parsnip liked the early morning the most.

He walked down the path until he reached the home of his best friend, Bertie Brontosaurus. She was a botanist, which Parsnip liked, because it was like being a scientist and an inventor but for plants. She'd even grown a new vegetable and named it after him.

The only downside was that the walk to get to Bertie was a long one, but this also meant Parsnip could complete his daily exercise. He knew exercise was extremely important for keeping both the mind and the body sharp. Bertie lived closer to Parsnip than anyone else did, but after the fire golem incident, Bertie had kindly suggested that Parsnip should have plenty of space around. That way his inventions could work as intended without interrupting anyone else by, say, crashing into someone's house and setting it on fire. Parsnip thought that sounded reasonable.

"Oh, hi there!" Bertie called, her long neck and high vantage point letting her see Parsnip when he was still far away.

Parsnip arrived properly a few minutes later and said, "Hi Bertie, how are things in the garden?"

"Always growing!" she replied. "That's what good gardens do!"

"When they have a wonderful gardener," Parsnip added with a grin.

Bertie smiled. "How's it coming with the Super Sprayer 6000? I'm so excited you're making a new watering system for me."

"It's the Super Sprayer 9000, now," he admitted. "And it's not going well. It's not super. It's not even spraying this time."

"Well, that won't do," Bertie said. She looked around her garden. "I have a few more things to plant here, so why don't you go pull the Super Sprayer 9000 outside, and we'll take a look at it together?"

Parsnip knew it would be no easy task to drag the machine outside, but Bertie couldn't fit into the cave very easily and Parsnip was always happier when Bertie was around. It was more fun to work on inventions together when they had the chance.

Parsnip walked home, enjoying the morning sunshine. When he got back to his cave, he unhooked the hoses and carefully pulled the contraption outside. When he laid it out, it looked like a flattened bug with a central metal pipe forming the spine and dozens of floppy hoses as legs. In theory, whenever he turned it on, water should flow through the spine of the machine and then the machine would regulate the water that came out of the hoses. In reality, though, there either wasn't enough water and nothing happened, or there was too much water and the hoses flopped and flew every which way—getting the entire world wet instead of just a garden. It was funny to see, but not very useful.

Bertie arrived and looked at the machine. "It looks like a flattened bug," she said.

"I was thinking the same thing!" Parsnip said with a laugh. "But I'm starting to wonder if I need a different design entirely."

"Maybe," Bertie said. "Can I see how it works? Or how it doesn't work?"

Parsnip appreciated that about Bertie. Like him, she understood that if you failed at something but still learned a thing or two in the process, it could be just as useful as succeeding. A failure wasn't a reason to give up; instead, it was a reason to try something else. Parsnip climbed back into the cave, running a hose from the water tank to the machine.

"Ready?" Parsnip called.

"Ready!" Bertie called back.

Parsnip pulled a lever and the water flowed out, slowly and without conviction. A few small bubbles came to the surface of the tank, but that was it.

"I don't see anything!" Bertie said. "Give it more power!"

Parsnip opened the valve to the tank a bit more.

"There's a bit of a trickle," Bertie yelled. "Give it all you've got!"

Parsnip spun the valve, opening it all the way. The tank gurgled and groaned and started draining rapidly.

"Oh, wow!" Bertie cried. "Amazing!" But then she followed it up with, "Turn it off, turn it off!"

Parsnip quickly shut the machine down, and after a few deep glugs and some giant bubbles rising to the surface, the tank quieted down as well. He climbed the ladder and opened the hatch to the cave, and water began to drip down over him. Not enough to be dangerous, but enough that he expected to have a very soggy yard indeed.

When he got outside, he was shocked. Bertie was soaked from head to toe, which was no small feat given how far apart Bertie's head and toes were in the first place. He thought she might be upset, which would be a completely reasonable response to being unexpectedly drenched. Bertie, however, was laughing enthusiastically.

"Well, that was certainly something," she said, shaking her head and sending water droplets flying. "What a good way to water a garden, as long as you're okay with watering the house, the gardener, and the tools all at the same time.

I bet we could water the moon, if we turned that thing up high enough!"

The Super Sprayer 9000 now looked less like a flattened bug and more like a bug that had gotten into a heroic wrestling match and most definitely lost. It was twisted and tangled every which way. Bertie, still dripping, was engaged in the task of straightening it all out again.

"That's the problem," Parsnip said. "Too much or too little pressure. Either nothing gets wet, or everything does."

Bertie looked it over. "I have an idea," she said. "I don't think your machine is broken enough."

"Huh?" Parsnip wondered. As far as he knew, his invention wasn't actually broken. It just didn't work exactly how he wanted it to.

Bertie pulled a small pointed trowel from her belt. "May I?" she asked.

"Go for it," Parsnip said.

Bertie set to work on one of the hoses, poking holes in it at regular intervals. "Go turn it on again. Maybe not full blast this time, but pretty powerful. Maybe three-quarters of the way?"

Parsnip climbed back down into his cave, making sure he was extra careful on the wet and slippery ladder. He was a hardheaded dinosaur, but he didn't want to test out just how hard his head truly was if he could help it. He went to the lever, turned the machine on again, and then opened the valve three-quarters of the way just like Bertie had suggested. There was another deep groan and another large gurgle, and Parsnip waited to see what would happen.

"Come out, come out!" Bertie yelled.

Parsnip scrambled back up the ladder and looked on in amazement as hoses flailed in every direction. Bertie tried to dodge sprays of water when she could, but there were far too many to avoid. But of all the parts flying every which way, the one part that caught Parsnip's attention was the one that wasn't moving. The hose that Bertie had poked with her trowel was on the ground. Water gushed from the end of the hose, but it also shot into the air in tiny streams from each of the holes that Bertie had poked in it.

"If I poke holes in all of the hoses and maybe close off the ends, you could water everything you needed to at once without getting water everywhere else," Parsnip said.

"And I could put some stakes next to the hose to keep it from moving!" Bertie said.

A spray of water hit Parsnip in the face, but he was so busy thinking about his invention that he barely noticed. "I could use washers to reinforce the small holes so they don't tear!"

Bertie lowered her head and gently bonked Parsnip with it, which was their personal version of a high-five. There was still water everywhere, so they enjoyed playing in it before they started cleaning up. Parsnip wasn't sure if this version of the Super Sprayer 9000 would work, but it felt like a very good idea. That was his favorite part of being an inventor: If you were smart, clever, persistent, and okay with getting a little help, there would be a moment where everything came together into something really great.

It works that way for everyone else too, even if they're not inventors.

A Job Too Big for a T-Rex?!

Tank the Tyrannosaurus never originally wanted to be a park ranger. When he was young, he'd imagined being a teacher or a nurse—maybe a carpenter—but it was hard to do those things with such small arms. To make it even harder, Tank was a very big dinosaur, even for a Tyrannosaurus, which made it hard to fit into places with other dinosaurs.

His dad, Tank Sr., showed him the outdoors. He showed him flowing rivers and flourishing forests and magnificent mountains, all beautiful and all in need of being taken care of. Tank and his father had the same idea: The outdoors needed protecting, and no one could be a better protector than a fierce, mighty, Tyrannosaurus rex. So Tank ended up becoming a park ranger.

Today, he thought, was going to be a long day. A Triceratops had told him that there was a monster out at the Tooth and Nail Tar Pit. Mind you, that Triceratops hadn't actually seen the monster; he'd just learned about the monster from his child.

He knew the journey through the jungle would be challenging for him, so he decided he would ask a friend of his to help him investigate this supposed tar pit monster. Afterward, they could meet up at their favorite donut shop and talk about how to handle the situation. The employees at the donut shop were always nice to him and gave him a pair of extra-long chopsticks so he could pick up the donuts with his tiny arms.

He headed over to his friend's store and looked at the sign: a white fox holding a magnifying glass. Purple letters underneath the fox read "Katey Kitsune Detective Agency." Another sign in the window read "No mystery too big—all mysteries solved, one low price." But when he got closer he saw there was another, newer sign on the door. It read "Permanently Closed. Off to new adventures. Thank you and much love, Katey."

Well, that wasn't ideal. Tank was going to have to investigate by himself, and that meant his donut would have to wait. It's tough to put off something you're looking forward to, but Tank took pride in being responsible.

The trip through the jungle was not an easy one. Tank had done it many times, but he still tripped over vines and tree stumps and got smacked in the face by low-hanging branches. Trekking through the jungle was his least favorite part of the job, but even if he didn't like doing it, it was still important. He wanted dinosaurs to be able to use the jungle, and that meant keeping it safe.

Eventually, he came to a path which was too small for him to walk along easily, but even a difficult-to-use path was better than nothing. He didn't see anyone while he was out walking and sort of wished he had brought someone with him. But if there really was a monster at the tar pit, maybe it was good that he was by himself and no one else would be in danger.

Up ahead, there was a sign on the path. It was hard to read at first, but when he got closer the words became clear: "Matey's Magnificent Munchies! Grand Opening!" Under the words, there was a picture of an Ankylosaurus dressed like a pirate. Under the picture, there was an arrow pointing down a different path.

If there was one thing any respectable Tyrannosaurus loved, it was munchies, and Tank was quite respectable if he did say so himself. He had a soft spot for pirates as well; his grandmother had been a pirate when she was younger.

But... Tank pulled his attention back to the tar monster. He needed to keep going. It disappointed him that it would be difficult to come back another day for munchies, but a Triceratops had reported the monster to him and now it was his job to look into it. Tank took his job very seriously.

Eventually the jungle started to thin out and became easier to travel through, with fewer trees and less underbrush. Soon the jungle stopped all together, and the Tooth and Nail Tar Pit came into view. He would have a look around, see that there was nothing out of the ordinary, and—

There it was. Giant, hulking, and full of spikes. A real tar monster. And it looked like it was in trouble.

The monster had hauled itself out of the tar pit, but it didn't get very far. Now it was lying on the beach, breathing heavily and still completely covered in the sticky black tar. With each deep breath, it looked like a heaving, living mountain, as black as the night sky.

Tank approached with caution. He was big even by dinosaur standards, but he felt like a child again next to this giant creature. He tried to get close to its head, to ask the monster how he could help. But when he came near, the monster growled at him. Tank leaped back. It didn't surprise him that the monster was not in a very good mood, but it did mean that he would need to be even more careful.

Tank circled back around behind the monster, avoiding the weakly thrashing tail. He tried to remove some of the tar, but it was incredibly sticky and still hot, even if it was rapidly cooling. His tiny arms made the task even more difficult, and he didn't know if he was supposed to be helping the monster get into the tar or get out of it.

"I know that when I'm feeling grumpy, I start with a healthy snack. Maybe that will help," Tank muttered to himself.

If he was being honest, he'd been craving snacks himself and wasn't too happy about putting them off to check on the tar pits. But he was glad he had, because now there might still be enough time to help the monster before it was too late.

Tank wasn't sure what tar monsters liked to eat. He found a giant, flat stone on the beach and dragged it toward the jungle. Once he was there, Tank began grabbing anything that looked edible. Bananas and bright flowers. Fresh leaves and giant figs. Sour berries, tough tree bark, and even some slithering slugs for good measure. He piled it all on the stone and carefully dragged it back to the monster. He had to stop and put things on again as they rolled, slid, or bounced off, but he was determined, and before long he made it back to where the monster was lying.

The monster growled at him again as he got close, but once it saw the pile of food behind Tank, the growling stopped. It opened its mouth and revealed a giant, thick, pink tongue. It was the first thing Tank had seen on the monster that wasn't covered in tar.

Tank stepped closer, pulling the stone behind him. He was slow and cautious, ready to jump away in a flash in case the monster decided *he* was the snack. Fortunately, the monster didn't snap at him, although it looked ready to do so if anything surprised it.

The moment the pile of food was close enough, the monster's giant tongue swept out. Tank leapt away and watched in surprise as the entire pile disappeared into the monster's mouth, slugs and all. The monster crunched happily and then swallowed. Tank was astonished. He loved snacks of all kinds and had been dreaming of donuts all day, but even he ate his snacks one at a time.

The monster's eyes closed, and Tank couldn't tell if it was awake or asleep. All he knew was that the monster still needed help. Tank had stayed focused, worked hard, and maybe even saved the monster's life. However, the monster still needed more help—help getting more food and water, along with getting clean. If Tank was going to finish rescuing the monster, he was going to need a lot of help, and he was going to need it fast. Thankfully, he had always been friendly and kind to others, so he knew he could find help when he needed it.

Although it was hard to put off having the donuts and potentially exciting new snacks he wanted, he was determined to stay focused on his duties as a park ranger and rescue the monster no matter what it took. Tank returned to the jungle, hurrying much faster this time. He would be back.

The Sea Turtle's Journey

A very long time ago, before even the dinosaurs walked on land, most creatures lived in the ocean. There were long-necked plesiosaurs and dolphin-like ichthyosaurs, sharks of all sizes, and any number of tiny swimming animals.

Zandelmandechar was the youngest mega-turtle in his family—a clan of giant sea turtles with massive spikes on their shells. When he was little, he had trouble saying his name, so everyone called him Zan. He rather liked the name Zan, so it stuck. Swimming through the ocean was one of his favorite things to do, and although he wasn't very good at it at first, he still had fun trying. Before long, though, he was zipping around with ease: gliding through currents, racing his brothers and sisters, and practicing flips and other tricks.

The only thing that bothered Zan about the ocean was that it always felt cold. His parents and his siblings thought that was a bit silly—maybe the ocean was cold, but it was what it was and you couldn't change it. It was where they lived. Zan understood that, but just because they had always lived in the ocean didn't make it comfortable.

Zan was not a small turtle for long. He kept growing, and by the time he was a teenager, he was bigger and spikier than his parents and much bigger than his older brothers and sisters. He was almost as big as his grandfather, whom everyone called Grandpa B. You may be wondering, Why did they call him Grandpa B? You see, his real name was twice as long as Zandelmandechar and *no one* in the family could pronounce it. Sea turtles really love giving each other long names.

One day, Zan had an idea. He had lived in the ocean with his family for his entire life, but the ocean was a very big place—what if, somewhere else, it was warmer? Then he could play and swim and race and be comfortable at the same time. He might even be able to meet new friends and find new and exciting wonders. The ocean was so big that he rarely saw anyone but his family, and he wondered what else might be out there.

His parents didn't like his idea. They had lived in this part of the ocean their whole lives as well, and they liked it here. Plus, they had no idea what the rest of the ocean might be like. What if it was dangerous, or dark, or even colder? Maybe the place they lived wasn't ideal, but it was good enough.

Grandpa B had other ideas. When he heard that Zan wanted to go exploring, he got a twinkle in his eye. No one ever asked Grandpa B what it was like when he was young, but before Grandpa B was a grandpa or even a dad, he was an explorer. Zan's parents may have lived in this part of the ocean their entire lives, but Grandpa B hadn't.

Grandpa B pulled Zan aside and whispered, "You know, I wasn't born here like you and your parents were."

Zan perked up immediately. He didn't know that. Since Grandpa B was so old, Zan had never imagined him doing anything else. He was gigantic, far larger than even Zan's parents, and the spikes on his shell were enormous. Mega-turtles grew their entire lives, and Grandpa B was the oldest turtle that Zan knew. Now, Zan started to wonder what his grandfather was like when he was young, so he let his grandpa continue on with his story.

"Where I grew up, the ocean was very dark. We could barely see anything at all. Sometimes fish would swim by and they would have a bit of a glow, but usually we could barely see our fins in front of our faces. And if you think it's cold here..." Grandpa B shivered.

"I get it," Zan moped. "Things are pretty good here, and I should be happy and get used to it."

"Absolutely not!" Grandpa B said with a laugh. "Just the opposite. I struck out on my own and I found a place I liked much better than where I was from. Going exploring made my life better, and later on made a better life for your parents, too."

"So you're saying... if I go exploring, my life will get better too?" Zan asked.

"Maybe, maybe not. You'll have to leave this place, which isn't perfect, but it's pretty comfortable. I'm too old to go with you, and I think your parents will want to stay here. I don't know about your brothers and sisters, but I don't think they're going anywhere either. You're the first person in the family who's thought about leaving," said Grandpa B.

That made Zan feel a little bit guilty. "So you're saying I'd have to go alone? What about the family?"

"Everyone in the family loves you very much," Grandpa B said. "And it's true, we would be sad if you left. But you should do what's best for you, and you can always come back to visit and tell us about your adventures."

Zan had a lot to think about. He was safe here and he loved his family. He didn't want to make them upset. A long time passed, and Zan got older. He got bigger, too, and soon he was bigger than even Grandpa B, and still growing. Grandpa B watched Zan grow up, always with that sparkle in his eye, but they didn't talk about traveling again. None of his siblings expressed any interest in exploring, and Zan felt like he should stay and help his family—especially since he was so big and strong.

He was still cold, though, and felt there was something better for him out there, although he liked being close to his family. The idea of being by himself was intimidating, and the idea of trying something new and being in an unfamiliar place was kind of scary. It was interesting and exciting too, but it was still scary nonetheless. He knew, though, that if he didn't go exploring, he would always wonder what would have happened if he went. This made him wonder if his mom and dad ever thought about things like that.

Grandpa B was the first to find out.

"I think I'm going to explore the sea," Zan told him. He already knew he was going and didn't like the way he had added *I think* to his statement. He was still nervous about how his family would react, though, so making it sound like he was unsure meant that he could see how they would respond.

"You think?" Grandpa B said. He was always good at knowing what was on Zan's mind.

"I'm going," Zan said more firmly.

"There you go," Grandpa B responded. "Don't feel bad about telling people what you plan to do. It's your decision, and no one knows you better than you do."

"I feel really certain," Zan explained. "Does that mean I'm making the right choice? Will I find something better?"

Grandpa B laughed again. "I don't know. Trying something doesn't guarantee success, young man, even when you really want it to. Two things are certain, though—you'll never know unless you try, and you'll always feel regret if you don't. Besides, you'll always have a place to come home to if it doesn't work out."

The words stuck in Zan's mind. *You never know unless you try.* He couldn't stand the idea of not knowing—of always wondering if he should have gone exploring or not. Grandpa B's words made Zan feel better about his upcoming journey, so he told his parents his plan. They were worried about him, of course, and told him he was welcome to stay as long as he liked. He understood that was their way of asking him not to go even if they didn't want to say so out loud, because they also wanted Zan to follow his heart.

His mother packed him some food and his father helped him inspect his shell and make sure he was strong and ready for the journey. They were worried about him, but they knew Zan had to chase his dream and they wanted to give him their support. They had a small farewell party, and then Zandelmandechar the Mega-turtle swam alone into the dark ocean.

At first, he swam upward. He had heard from other fish that the world was brighter up there but also more dangerous, because anything could see you whenever they wanted, even from far away. But Zan was huge and still growing every day, and his shell was covered in spikes and as strong as armor. He saw a few scary-looking animals—sharks with jagged teeth and round fish full of spines—but they left him alone. He thought, because he was so big, maybe they were just as nervous around him as he would be around them. He gave them a lot of distance in return to avoid scaring anyone.

Eventually, he made it to the surface, which was a new and exciting experience for him. The not-water was warm on his skin, and there was a great glowing orb in the sky that made him even warmer. (Later, he would learn these things were called "air" and "the sun," although they were new to him now.)

He swam through the ocean with his great and powerful legs until, for the first time, he saw something that was not the ocean. He was too curious not to have a look, and he climbed onto a sandy thing that he learned was called a "beach." The sand was delightfully hot, and Zan rolled around in it, happy and warm. He felt like the journey had been a success, and he was proud.

Night soon fell, though, which cooled the sand. It made Zan uncomfortable, since it was dry and a bit scratchy. He went back into the ocean to rinse off, but when he returned to the beach, the sand stuck to him again. It was unavoidable. He still liked it more than his home in the ocean, but he thought, *If I've succeeded so far, why not keep trying?* He got a good night's sleep, then decided to venture into the forest.

It was a strange world. Creatures he couldn't see made all manner of sounds— howling, growling, buzzing, chirping, and singing—that were new, wonderful, and a little bit scary. Zan was not graceful as he walked. He crashed through the woods, knocked over trees, and trampled bushes. A few curious critters came to watch the commotion, but for the most part, they stayed away.

Zan liked the jungle. It was hot and damp from all the trees and rainfall, and it didn't have as much scratchy dry sand as the beach. But, even though it was better than the beach and the beach was better than the ocean, he felt like if he kept going, he could find somewhere even better where he could really make a new home.

After days of walking, Zan began to worry. He was now far from the ocean and wasn't sure about finding his way back if he wanted to return. He had tried his best, but Zan was starting to think it wasn't going to be enough. However, he had set out to find a new home, and he wasn't going to give up easily. Even if he ended up having to return to his family and his old home in the ocean, first he wanted to know he had given it his all.

On the last day before Zan was going to admit defeat, the jungle suddenly cleared, revealing a hot, smoky, bubbling tar pit. He had never seen one before, and there were no other animals around. The tar pit might be dangerous for them, but Zan trusted his thick, leathery skin that had kept him safe in the cold, dark ocean. He dipped in a toe and found the tar to be... perfect.

Zan splashed into the tar pit and sank down. His body felt warmer than ever before, and the bubbles were soothing and relaxing after such a long journey. Zan didn't think he could breathe in the tar like he could underwater, so he had to stick his head out occasionally for some air, but he had finally found the perfect home. He was so glad he didn't give up and he settled in for a nice, relaxing tar bath.

The Great Sky Rescue

Aerothea the Great sailed through the air on her giant wings. She was a Quetzalcoatlus, the largest flying animal who ever lived. Because she was so big and needed so much room to fly around, she had chosen to make her nest in an isolated spot outdoors. Now, though, her nesting site was anything but isolated.

The dinosaurs below looked small from so high in the air, but the one thing that was for sure was that there were a lot of them. A Tyrannosaurus was giving orders to the dinosaurs around him, and a small army of Stegosauruses ran back and forth between the jungle and the tar pit, all carrying food. A family of Triceratops tried their best to keep the children on task and out of trouble. There was even a dinosaur with some sort of strange, water-spraying contraption.

It was a fiasco, and her eggs were somewhere right in the middle of it.

Aerothea floated down slowly in circles, trying to make sense of the commotion. There was some sort of giant creature covered in tar at the center of it. It ate the food that the Stegosauruses brought from the jungle, and the tar was getting washed off with the water-spraying contraption—although that part did not appear to be going well, since none of the dinosaurs could reach the top of the creature even while it was laying down. Besides, even if they could reach the top, the spikes on the creature's shell could easily injure them.

It looked like a sea turtle, but that couldn't be right—it was much too big, and it had giant spikes on its shell. Aerothea went to the ocean often in search of fish. (That was why she was away from her eggs in the first place.) She had seen a lot of sea turtles, some of them very large, but none like this. This must be the oldest, biggest sea turtle that had ever lived, or perhaps it was some kind of relative to the sea turtles that none of the dinosaurs had encountered before.

A few of the dinosaurs looked up at her as she glided down and landed softly, but most were too busy to pay her any attention. She noticed immediately that not only were her eggs missing, but her entire nest was gone.

She was scared. She was angry. She already made it a habit to avoid other dinosaurs when she could, and now they were here *and* her eggs were missing. Aerothea didn't care about anything else.

With a powerful flap of her wings, she took to the air and flew straight for the Tyrannosaurus rex, who appeared to be in charge.

"I don't know what all of you are doing here," Aerothea said. "But you need to give me back my eggs, and then you all need to leave. This is my home and you are trespassing."

Tank the Tyrannosaurus looked momentarily panicked. He didn't think they had fed any eggs to the tar monster, but there was a lot going on. If there were eggs around somewhere, he had no idea where to find them.

"Hello, Miss!" he called to the impressively large creature. He was running into a lot of those today. "I'm afraid I haven't seen any eggs around, but there is an awful lot going on right now."

"Yes," Areothea said dryly. "That is the problem. There's a whole wide world out there, and all of you decided to be right here together. Never a good idea, I say."

If the Tyrannosaurus was still listening to her, he didn't show it. He was directing a group of Stegosauruses who were hauling a vine full of watermelons out of the jungle. Was that... paint on their plates? It made sense, Aerothea supposed. It was so difficult to tell land dinosaurs apart.

A Pachycephalosaurus wearing a white coat and a hard hat ran over them. "Excuse me, Miss?" he asked. "Could I have your help? I have a job that is perfect for you."

"My name is Areothea. And no, you may not."

Aerothea flew higher into the air to get a better look around and to get away from the dinosaur who wanted her help. Could you imagine? A Quetzalcoatlus working together with all these other creatures. Ridiculous. She worked alone, and that's how she liked it.

Down on the ground, a Triceratops was waving to her, trying to get her attention. She was going to ignore the little thing, since she had more important things to worry about, but then she noticed something. A teeny, tiny, flying animal was with the Triceratops, buzzing around excitedly. It couldn't be... Could it? She flew like lightning to where they were standing.

"Hi!" the Triceratops said. "We found this Pterodactyl hatchling here, and took his nest and the other eggs home to keep them safe from the tar monster. Except it wasn't a monster. It was just a very big turtle, and now we are here to help. The eggs hatched and ruined our house and—"

Aerothea ignored the child, who appeared ready to continue talking until it ran out of air and almost passed out. She inspected the hatchling closely.

"Toodles!" it said.

"What on earth and sky is a Toodles?" Aerothea asked.

The Triceratops child, who was still talking, stopped mid-sentence to answer the question. "That's his name! Toodles the Pterodactyl."

Aerothea's eyes narrowed. "Ridiculous. And anyway, that hatchling is not a Pterodactyl. It is a Quetzalcoatlus. *My* Quetzalcoatlus hatchling, in fact. Where are the others, egg thief?"

"Egg rescuer," the Triceratops corrected helpfully. "I'm Tracer, and my friend Stinger is with the rest of them. They hatched, though. They aren't eggs anymore."

Aerothea looked around and saw a young Styracosaurus coming their way. He was holding some sort of bucket with a colander on top. From inside, Aerothea could hear more than a few squawks and squeaks, all competing for attention.

"The two of you saved my babies? Working together?" Aerothea asked.

"Toodles helped too!" Tracer volunteered. "And my mom and dad. Taking care of hatchlings is awfully hard work."

"I am grateful," Aerothea said. She was proud, but she knew when someone had helped her.

"We couldn't have done it alone!" Tracer said. "Just like today. Everyone is pitching in to help the turtle and—"

The boy was winding up to start talking again, so Aerothea took to the air at once. It was her turn to pay back the favor, and she knew what she should do. Maybe, just this once, she could work together with the other dinosaurs instead of trying to do everything herself. She flew back to the Pachycephalosaurus in the white coat, who was fussing over a strange machine.

"I can help you now," Aerothea proclaimed. "I apologize for my earlier rudeness. You see, I was quite shocked by the commotion and busy looking for my hatchlings. They're safe because some dinosaurs helped out and worked together, and I would like to reciprocate."

The dinosaur roared in delight.

"Okay, here's how it works," he said excitedly. It sounded like this was his first chance to see his machine in action, although Aerothea correctly guessed that washing tar off a sea turtle was not the contraption's original purpose. "When the water turns on, there's going to be a lot of pressure. It will take someone mighty and strong to hold it still enough. And it has to get up into the air, to clean the top of the turtle. We ran a hose to a river and my friend Bertie is there to keep everything in place. That way—"

"Land dinosaurs sure do talk a lot when they are excited," Aerothea said. "But you don't need to worry, for I am mighty and strong and able to hold the machine still. And I can fly and reach the top of the turtle. I will carry it for you."

Aerothea took to the sky. The machine was much heavier than she thought it would be, and she struggled as she flapped her great wings. But she had all the land dinosaurs counting on her, so she used all of her strength to lift the machine in the air over the turtle. She looked down and saw the other dinosaurs all looking at her. The hoses on the machine dangled like jellyfish tentacles while everyone cheered.

The Pachycephalosaurus cranked a lever and Aerothea held on with all her might. The machine jerked her across the sky, this way and that, but she held on. Water got on the back of the turtle, on the ground, and on the other dinosaurs. They cheered even more, enjoying the cool water after a long, hot day of work. The tar melted away, and the giant sea turtle began to move more comfortably. Looking down at all their joy and excitement and success, Aerothea thought perhaps it wasn't so bad working with other dinosaurs after all. There was, in fact, something rather unexpectedly nice about working together as a group to help another creature.

Leave Your Feedback on Amazon

Please think about leaving some feedback via a review on Amazon. It may only take a moment, but it really does mean the world for small businesses like mine.

Even if you did not enjoy this title, please let us know the reason(s) in your review so that we may improve this title and serve you better.

From the Publisher

Hayden Fox's mission is to create premium content for children that will help them expand their vocabulary, grow their imaginations, gain confidence, and share tons of laughs along the way.

Without you, however, this would not be possible, so we sincerely thank you for your purchase and for supporting our company mission.